The Christ Chronicles

by

Richard Moody Jr.

PITTSBURGH, PENNSYLVANIA 15222

The contents of this work including, but not limited to, the accuracy of events, people, and places depicted; opinions expressed; permission to use previously published materials included; and any advice given or actions advocated are solely the responsibility of the author, who assumes all liability for said work and indemnifies the publisher against any claims stemming from publication of the work.

All Rights Reserved
Copyright © 2011 by Richard Moody Jr.

No part of this book may be reproduced or transmitted, downloaded, distributed, reverse engineered, or stored in or introduced into any information storage and retrieval system, in any form or by any means, including photocopying and recording, whether electronic or mechanical, now known or hereinafter invented without permission in writing from the publisher.

RoseDog Books
701 Smithfield Street
Pittsburgh, PA 15222
Visit our website at *www.rosedogbookstore.com*

ISBN: 978-1-4349-8559-0
eISBN: 978-1-4349-7554-6

Part I

Introduction

In Retrospect: Always Challenge My Teachings

Pain. A dull, throbbing pain punctuated by the sting of thorns as they dig into my scalp at each lurching step; the feel of wood on raw wounds from the lash and the incessant flies. Under the crushing weight of the cross, I stumble and fall. Another stumble; an old woman offers me a drink from a bowl. It tastes vile.

"Crone! Why do you torment me with this bitter water?"

"Lord, this is the sweetest water you will ever drink," she replied.

Instantly I knew why she did what she did. "Bless you, my child."

The soldier whipped me again, and I moved in a trance toward my horrible fate. Lashed to the cross, I saw why the process of crucifixion is a sign of the fundamental bestiality of man. Death that God gave Adam and Eve is now a welcome visitor.

In my delusions, Satan visited me on the cross and showed me what Christians would do in my name. I knew that Satan had no reason to lie to me. I saw men with crosses on metal disks and swords, slaughtering innocent men, women, and children. I saw men and women screaming in agony as their tormentors pulled them apart by their limbs. I saw the slaughter of a pious people and, worst of all, a man in strange clothing with a mustache. He ordered the extermination of my people. I saw thousands of emaciated people living in squalor. In anguish I called out in horror,

"Forgive them, Father, for they know not what they do!" I was referring not to the Romans who crucified me, not to some of the Jews who persecuted me, but to my own followers.

Chapter 1

Oblivion at last; and I didn't even feel the lance piercing my side. Consciousness resumed, and I found myself in this dark tunnel with a brilliant glow at the end. I could feel faith, hope, and love washing over me. Then a voice; my mother, Mary, cried out to me. "Jesus! Step out of the tunnel and join me for eternity!"

"A mother or father who loves his son or daughter more than me is unworthy of me. A child who loves his parents more than he loves me is unworthy of me." Be gone voices! I fainted, but not before saying, "Father, I have returned."

As I drifted off, a voice said to me, "Not yet. There is still work to be done."

Chapter 2

Suddenly I am in a sarcophagus. The excruciating pain forces me to crawl on my elbows and knees towards a flicker of light along the wall. Using all my might, I push aside a boulder blocking the entrance and crawl out. Mary, my mother, and Mary Magdalene, my wife, are holding vigil and are catatonic with suppressed emotion. They caress me and rush to find wine to dull the pain and bandages to bind my wounds. Gently they pick me up under my armpits and stumble away, but not before rolling the boulder back in place. They find a good place to hide for the remainder of the day, and then we venture out at night, allowing me to limp to the outskirts of the village.

Later that morning, the Apostles are stunned by my presence as I sit on a boulder. They rush to embrace me and I ask each one: "Am I alive or are you talking to a shadow? Touch my wounds to see if I am flesh and blood."

Each Apostle touches me to see if I am really a person and not a ghost. "Now you must leave. I have a different fate my Father has chosen for me. Spread the word of my resurrection. I have not only raised Lazarus, but my Father has raised me from the dead."

The Apostles leave reluctantly.

I say to my mother, Mary, and my wife, Mary, "We cannot stay here. While it would be a tremendous surprise for me to reappear, it is faith, not reality, which matters. I must go into seclusion. Where is the nearest leper colony? They are outcasts and will harbor a fugitive. Please bandage my hands and feet, and help me get to the leper colony."

Chapter 3

It is now dusk, and the three of us spot what looks like a leper colony. I see an elderly man and ask him, "Can you help us? We are outcasts and need your assistance." The lepers find me a small ledge in the cave with some straw to permit me to lie down. I order my wife and mother to leave; they need to spread the gospel. I notice a dark, lean man whose face is difficult to read. Is he smiling at me or mocking me? "I am Swadu, the village scribe."

As he introduces himself, I feel a little uneasy. "Swadu, here is a small sack of food; please share it with those most in need. How do you provide food and water to your people?"

"We have garden plots and the Good Samaritans provide us with supplies. We have bread and olives in the morning, milk, and occasionally goat meat in the evening."

"Swadu, are you really are a scribe?"

"Why do you doubt me?"

"No reason; it's just that scribes are difficult to find and finding one in a leper colony seemed unusual."

"Even scribes get leprosy."

Oh, wondrous event! Someone who can record my thoughts, keep them secret and, I hope, give them to my followers (or should I say joiners). My disciples didn't just follow me; they actively participated in the many debates we had about God, such as the meaning of life and why our magnificent Father works in such profound ways.

"When I recover from my wounds, would you write down some ideas I have had?"

"What possible things of interest could a common outcast have?"

"I am something of a philosopher; please humor me."

Swadu laughs. "Do you really think you have any ideas worth preserving?"

"Perhaps not; you be the judge. For now I must rest."

Chapter 4

Four days pass and my wounds are infected. Writhing in bed, sweating profusely, I ask a pretty, young girl if she can give me some wine to dull the pain. She returns with the wine and whispers to me, "Swadu is dark in spirit. Be careful; he is brilliant, but he will twist your mind. You can't take everything he has to say at face value. He appears to have a troubled past and a bleak outlook toward the future."

"Swadu, are you a healer, too?" I ask.

"My talents here have been used to help other lepers."

"What can you do?"

"Close your eyes," he says.

I feel a jarring blow to my face and then lapse into an unconscious state. Unknown to me, Swadu put a metal rod into the fire, heated it red hot, and then used the poker to burn out the bad flesh.

The next day, I awake and scream in pain, but my fever is over. Not knowing if I would live or die, I ask Swadu if he would write down my thoughts. When I was on the cross, I described what Satan had showed me. The terrible things my followers would do in my name were profoundly depressing. It is not too late; maybe I can prevent the terrible transgressions my followers will commit in my name.

"Swadu, I fear that those who believe in me will do terrible things if I do not set limits on what they do. So I say this to them: 'Never strike a blow to further my name, for it is me you strike.' Also, 'Lead by example, not by force of will'

"So you acknowledge that your teachings will be misinterpreted; that you make mistakes?" Swadu asks.

"Everyone makes mistakes," I reply.

"Even God?"

"God made only one mistake. He trusted Lucifer."

"Was it trust, or was God just naïve?" he asks.

5

"God must have assumed that no one would try to dominate the heavenly host. It would appear that Lucifer had the human quality of aggression. God could not believe that Lucifer would act on that aggression."

"Is Hell the act of a reasonable being? This strikes me as the most vengeful act imaginable. How can you justify such a horrible fate for those who don't believe as you believe?"

"So you believe that I am Jesus?" I ask.

"Yes. How else could you have survived crucifixion?"

"So a common criminal could not survive crucifixion?"

"No," he replies. "I asked about Hell; Jesus, you are a hypocrite. First you preach the need for peace, love, and the need to forgive your enemies. Then you condemn all who disagree with you to the most horrible fate imaginable. Why should your followers not regard you as a hypocrite?"

I laugh. "Hell is not a literal fate. It is an attempt by me to prove to my followers — or joiners, if you prefer — that I make mistakes to prove I am human. After all, I am first and foremost The Son of Man, a mortal, and the Son of God, an immortal. My mortal acts are my mistakes; my immortal acts are my miracles performed in the service of God."

Swadu is unconvinced. "If you preach the ability to forgive, do you accept God's punishment of Adam and Eve? They were two, innocent children who were led astray by the most evil creature in existence. Why did God enact the most brutal punishment upon them?"

"God gave them the kindest gift of all: death in earthly form and eternal life in spiritual form. God said to Adam, 'Trust Me; have faith in Me.' Satan said to Eve, 'Listen to Me.' Satan used logic to destroy faith. That is original sin. It was important for Adam and Eve to know for all eternity that the first time logic was ever used, it was used for evil.

"While logic is neither good nor evil, evil men will use it to justify cruel and unspeakable acts. This would never happen if revelation, trust, faith, and intuition serve as the source of wisdom and judgment. Experience is necessary for good judgment, provided that the individual is aware that any information derived from the physical world is suspect. That is why any system of laws derived through experiences from the physical world is a potential source of evil.

"Those who try to find truth in the physical world will be perpetually confused. Since the physical world is partly the corpus of Satan, then the physical world will lie, and lie, and lie to those naïve enough to believe that the physical world is the true, unambiguous representation of reality. Only those who have faith in both the spiritual world and the physical world have any ability to distinguish truth from the lies told to them by the physical world.

"At the time of creation, good and evil came into existence together as God willed Himself into existence in the spiritual world. God did not realize, however, that a countervailing presence — Satan — also willed himself into existence, only in the physical world. They both annihilated each other creating the physical and spiritual worlds you see around us, which are part good, part evil.

"But the one thing that Satan must accept logically is that if God starts to lose the battle, He will rely on faith and hope he will win.

"If Satan starts to lose, what does he do? Rely on despair? No, he must have hope that he will win. This weakens him because hope is always good, even though the object of that hope may be evil.

"Suppose that God and Satan were evenly matched for eternity, and God starts to lose. What does He do? Rely on hope. If Satan starts to lose and relies on hope, it weakens him. The more he begins to have hope, the more he weakens himself. He must, as the supreme logician, accept defeat. This supreme logician originates in the physical world.

"The physical world is slowly being converted into the spiritual world as it passes through the guts of the good, spiritual world. The evil spiritual world is consumed as food by the good, spiritual world. Good incrementally increases and, slowly, the physical world evaporates. When the process is complete, only the good, spiritual world will exist; except, of course, if the spiritual world decides to take physical expression.

"This is, however, fraught with danger because there is no knowing the precise fate that will befall anyone reentering the physical world."

"How long will this process take?" Swadu asks.

"This will take as long as this world, and every other world, is converted into the good, spiritual world. This will take an eternity."

"Isn't that a convenient attitude to justify God's lack of omniscience and omnipotence?" Swadu challenges.

"God is neither omniscient nor omnipotent; this is common fallacy," I reply.

"How can God then know the future?"

"Your question has no meaning. The past, present, and future are all merged together so that all wisdom is potentially achievable."

Swadu seems to be confused. "Then God is omniscient after all?"

"No. God does not have complete knowledge of the physical world. Satan can still provide unpleasant surprises like floods, earthquakes, famine, and so forth. God only knows the spiritual world with wisdom approaching omniscience. What the precise nature of the interaction between the spiritual world and the physical world is something of a mystery to God.

"Omniscience was always a specious concept. If we could compel God to do a task that God would see no reason to do, why would God do it even though He could do it? Why would God want to count every grain of sand in the sea?"

"So this automatically means that God is not omnipotent?" Swadu inquires.

"Precisely," I respond.

I continue, "You have to remember that God said He was the Alpha and the Omega; the beginning and the end. He never said he was the middle. This is the middle; the journey to eternal happiness and love. We experience this now in all-too-fleeting moments. But as the physical world succumbs to the spiritual world, we must ultimately see around us — despite increasing waves of despair, depravity, hatred, and violations of God's laws — hope, morality, love, and obedience to God's laws."

"You say obedience to God's laws. Why should we be obedient to God's laws? Adam and Eve died for the right to have free will. Now God shows up in the vehicle of Moses and, in a supreme act of duplicity, takes away this right by imposing a set of laws upon us. In effect God is saying to humanity, 'You are too brutish and ignorant to come up with your own moral, legal, and ethical codes, so I will dictate them to you.' We died for the right to have free will and now God takes it away from us with the Ten Commandments."

Getting slightly annoyed, I say, "Life is a cord joining generations. Cut the cord and the baby is free to choose. Wrong choices mean that generations of wisdom are lost forever. The freedom to choose does not include the freedom to choose evil."

"How then can we be free, if not free to do evil?" Swadu asks.

"God will not allow us to wallow in our own filth. Timeless wisdom cannot be overturned by freedom of choice. The laws of Moses handed down by God restrict freedom, but appeal to a broader wisdom. To suggest that the individual can choose to violate these laws by virtue of will is dangerous. Just as God, our Father, does not permit us to do evil, secular and religious law places limits on our behavior. Religious laws proscribe behavior not already prohibited expressly in the Ten Commandments.

"Swadu, what would you offer as an alternative?" I ask.

"A set of laws derived from man by experience, logic, and reason," he answers.

"What you are proposing is chaos. As soon as man is free to choose his own laws, he will choose whatever laws suit his immediate needs. Hungry? Just pass a law outlawing the harboring of grains so that every individual gets an equal amount. Want to commit murder? Just specify whatever crimes you wish to satisfy the requirement of the death sentence, and do it in the name of the state. How about permitting theft if it is to avoid starvation or bearing false witness to support a friend?

"Take the Lord's name in vain? Why stop there? Why not just declare any statement by anyone is acceptable? This ensures the fundamental loss of civility in society. Loss of civility leads to anarchy as each individual pursues whatever whim suits him in the moment; even if it means antagonizing everyone around him. This can only lead to greater discord and strife. How is this beneficial to the individual?

I continue, "Individual rights involve individual responsibility. Failure to exercise that responsibility merits the loss of rights."

Unmoved, Swadu replies, "This all sounds great, but I still maintain that a system of laws derived from experience, honed in practice, brilliantly derived, and based on logic and reason are better than some set of delusions supposedly coming from God."

"So you think that man is smarter than God?" I ask.

"I don't trust the prophet system. The idea that a bunch of delusional men hearing God and then handing down his wisdom from on high is rife with potential corruption. What if the prophet lacks integrity? What if the price of the prophet's decisions is to expose others to extreme anguish?"

"All prophets have integrity and would never needlessly expose others to anguish."

Now Swadu stuns me. "Adam and Eve were the first prophets, yet they were deceived by Satan. Why should lesser prophets fare any better?"

"Your observation is troubling," I reply. "If we are to believe the story of Adam and Eve, then we must believe that Satan can perform miracles, too; in the case of Adam and Eve the miracle of talking as a snake. Since there no other accounts of animals talking to man, we must hope that prophets can distinguish between miracles from God and deceptions from Satan."

Swadu smirks and then asks, "Should women be obedient to God's laws?"

"Why do you ask this absurd question?"

"Which commandment says, 'Thou shall never commit rape'?"

A bit uneasy, I respond, "Just because there are no specific prohibitions against certain actions, that doesn't mean they are permitted."

He persists. "Where are the Commandments against rape, incest, arson, treason, and kidnapping? Don't these merit inclusion in the Ten Commandments?"

Seeing I am making no progress, I persist. "The laws handed down by God put limits on man's behavior. The most important law is: 'Never take the name of the Lord thy God in vain.'"

Swadu snorts. "Why doesn't God just develop a thicker skin? Isn't it a sad commentary about God that He places such importance on defaming Him that it surpasses even, 'Thou shall not commit murder' in importance?"

Point taken, I say to myself. "Taking the name of the Lord thy God in vain is not about God. It is about limits and the fundamental relationship between God, us, and our communities. While murder is offensive, isn't it even more offensive that we view God as so trivial that we can thwart His will whenever we choose to by defaming Him? Once blasphemy becomes commonplace, the believers will begin to doubt why they should have faith in a God that permits the non-believers to denigrate and demean him."

"Nonsense," says Swadu. He continues, "Where is the Devine retribution for such blasphemy? If there is no Hell, what fate awaits the non-believers? What happens to really evil individuals? Are they allowed to enter the Kingdom of Heaven eventually? How do you define evil?"

I am beginning to sense that I am losing this sparring match. "The greatest evil is the use of logic to destroy faith. Truly evil people are those who will go out of existence for eternity in terms of their spiritual persona, but will re-enter the physical world where they will serve as food for the spiritual world.

Once they become part of the spiritual world by assimilation, they can repent or keep going through this cycle until they see the error of their ways. There is no divine retribution for the non-believers; those that don't believe in the afterlife will, when they die, get the option of going out of existence for eternity." We must continue this discussion another time, Swadu, as now I am tired."

"Good evening, Jesus."

Chapter 5

Days pass and my wounds begin to heal, but it is still excruciating to walk or feed myself. Fortunately a pretty girl named Mary has taken me under her wing. She is tall and slender, but the signs of leprosy are evident as her hands and feet are being ravished by the disease. Still she has a wonderful soul and spirit that carries me through on my own, dark days.

I can tell Swadu is in the mood for another verbal joust, and I welcome his attempts to turn me into a cynic. Why waste time trying to convert the converted? I feel that my Father has destined for the two of us to cross paths. To his credit (or curse!), Swadu is persistent and tries to convince me of the fundamental evil of my Father.

I decide to start the battle. "You mention the absence of rape in the Ten Commandments. An oversight, to be sure, but any good system of laws has to start somewhere. God spoke to Moses and gave him the fundamentals of the Law. Clearly these are not the only Commandments that should be obeyed."

Swadu replies, "This wisdom seems fully in keeping with a stone mason's efforts. What did Moses feel in the presence of God? Fear. Isn't that deplorable? God, the most powerful being in the universe, deigns to speak to a man, and what does He do? Instill fear in the child.

"Moses was a child to God's adult. Why did God instill in Moses fear? Why not hope, joy, wonderment, amazement, happiness, or love? Why fear? And then God puts Himself first. If we look objectively at God, can we determine that He is good? Can we look at the Ten Commandments and say they are in the best interests of humanity?"

Now annoyed, I ask, "What would you prefer?"

"A set of clearly defined dos and don'ts that is unambiguous. Number one: Don't kill people or animals needlessly; Number two: Never force a woman to engage in intercourse who refuses to do so voluntarily; Number three: Never commit treason, arson, or kidnapping; Number four: 'Do unto others as they would have them do unto you' is too wordy. Why not just say, Be nice? That way you don't put yourself in the center of the universe; Number five:

Don't lie, cheat, or steal; and Number six: Don't honor any God who doesn't deserve to be honored. As I indicated earlier, the only good thing we got out of the Garden of Eden was the ability to have free will. God requires obedience but, when we talk about God's wisdom being beyond our understanding, we should submit to a candid world the true nature of your Father. Surely, Jesus, your teachings must first start with repudiating the excesses of your Father."

Now he is really rolling. "Let's start with the story of Job. What kind of monster would do to Job what God did to Job? The difference between a reasonable being and God is this: Suppose a bully shows up at your house one day and says to you, 'Do you mind if I torture your son to see if he will remain loyal to you?' Wouldn't an appropriate response be: 'If you touch one hair on the head of my son, I will beat you to within an inch of your life? Get out of here and never come back?

"Imagine you are Satan and wish to torment Job. Do you go up to God and tell Him you want to torment Job? He will tell you no. Now suppose we increase the stakes and tell God, 'Your man Job isn't very loyal; given half a chance, he will renounce his loyalty to you.'

"God replies, 'Job would never renounce his loyalty to me.' So Satan says, 'Do you mind if I torment him to test his loyalty to you?' And God says, 'Go right ahead; we must test Job's loyalty.' Think of Satan's brilliance! He knew that if he went to God to get to torment Job, that God would say no, so he comes up with this ingenious scheme to torment Job and got God's blessing to do it!"

"You are dark in spirit, Swadu, but do you really think that you are smarter than God? A possibility that you may have not considered is this: Was God powerless to stop Satan from tormenting Job? Suppose the war in heaven with Lucifer was far more destructive than we imagined, and heaven was destroyed and chaos set in. What if we, the direct descendants of God, are reshaping heaven in our own image? The destruction of heaven and hell occurred. Obviously, if God could create the earth, He could destroy heaven and hell, and so could Lucifer. What if Lucifer was cornered for eternity? What would he do? He would try to destroy everything around him in an insane act. Lucifer is not evil; he is merely insane, an insane God. Why would any rationale being reject God's love?"

Swadu disagrees. "A rational being would not be led around by the nose of those who profess to be superior to others by virtue of some perceived access to God. Have you ever considered what happened after Adam and Eve? We started out with direct communication with God, not hearsay. What do we have now? A system of religion in which we have you, the Son of Man and the Son of God, and the Apostles, your students, and your followers all doing 'God's' wishes. Don't you see where we are going? We will have a progressive religious structure designed to bring us closer to God when, in fact, it does just the opposite.

"Look at religion as a wedge separating God from humanity. The more ornate the religion, the more the average individual is separated from God. Why should we honor any religion that professes to teach us about God, when its real motive is to establish a structure to enrich those at the top of the religious ladder?

"Any truly religious individual should forsake any material goods, no matter what justification is given to justify wealth in the physical world; otherwise we have the very real possibly that self-enrichment supplants the desire to do God's wishes. Humanity needs guidance, not oppression. To teach that disagreement with God is instantly evil is to deny humanity any right of free will.

"Why does God work in *mysterious* ways? Why not promote rationality that meshes the thoughts of the religious individuals who support you, but also those that oppose you?"

I simply say, "You seem to forget. I told you that my Apostles and I have had lively discussions. Thomas clearly did note take everything I said at face value. Just because we had discussions doesn't mean, because we disagree, he is evil. There is no reason to suggest that God would do anything evil. In fact, He would never do anything that *appears* to be evil."

"I find these tests of faith, including that of Abraham and Job, to be demonstrable in other ways. Is it really *good* for God to require a test of faith that damages others who have not been permitted to respond to this test of faith? Was Abraham's test of faith any more important than Isaac's test of faith? Did God test the faith of Isaac when he tested Abraham's faith? For Abraham it was God's test of faith. For Isaac it was a test of faith in his father, not God."

Swadu responds, "Aha, I have caught you in a logical flaw. If children initially believe their parents are God, doesn't that mean that if an adult starts believing in God they, too, will begin to outgrow the need for God?"

"Swadu, look; we can disagree about the wisdom of God being transmitted to Mankind though prophets, but you must believe there are some things that cannot be explained by the mere presence of the physical world. We can be kind, considerate, faithful, loving, and compassionate individuals. Show me how this can happen in the physical world."

Chapter 6

Unbeknownst to me, Swadu, like Judas, betrayed me. He told me out of a sense of guilt that he had gone to the local authorities and sold me to them for a paltry sum. I cannot fault him for this, but I can fault him for the fact that he put others in jeopardy. Knowing my time was limited I decided to engage Swadu once again. It was fun engaging him in conversation. It forces me to question and then strengthens my faith in my Father. Clearly we were meant to meet.

What Swadu is writing is a mystery. I decide to ask Swadu what he is thinking. "What is your latest attempt to deny the existence of God?"

"Let's start with your *miracles*," he says. "Can you think of any rational reason why they could occur without being miracles?"

This is an interesting question, so I start to think of how these could occur in the absence of miracles. "Those who don't believe I raised Lazarus from the dead could argue that he was never dead. How do we know he was dead? In other words, raising Lazarus from the dead would require absolute certainty he was dead initially. How can we prove that?

"Walking on water was clearly a miracle, but skeptics could argue I was merely skipping on rocks just below the surface. Although I have no knowledge of sorcery, sorcerers can turn water into wine, so that is not proof of my divinity.

"Also, God did not part the Red Sea in any way that could be considered a miracle. Blowing the water out of the Sea of Reeds would allow Moses to pass to the other side with light, hand-pulled wagons. They could struggle through the mud. Pharaoh's troops, with more armor and heavy chariots, would have been mired in the mud, unable to escape; they would have steadily drowned. But isn't it a sign of God's wisdom that Moses could lead the Egyptians into the Sea?

"The destruction of Sodom was from the terrible disease afflicting them from their grotesque fornication. They would have gone insane and burned down their own cities, much as Nero did. Lot's wife turning to salt? Any time you have walked through the desert you will notice how badly cuts sting when you walk in certain areas. I have licked the ground and it is salty. Suppose Lot's wife had fallen into a crevasse, screamed as she fell, and Lot only saw a lump of salt that sort of looked like her when he looked over his shoulder. If he didn't notice the crevasse nearby, he might not have known she had fallen into the crevasse.

"John the Baptist noticed that by immersing himself in water, he could quell the demons in his mind. When you have to swim, breathe, and feel cold water, you can escape the horrors of your own mind. Later John thought this was a sign from God and began to convince others to partake of the beneficial needs of water. It started out, essentially, as way to achieve sanity. Later it became a cleansing ritual."

"I have doubts about the flood in Noah's time," says Swadu. "Why would God only kill the animals of the land? Would the fish die in the flood? Why are animals living in the water? Why would they be unaffected by the flood and survive, while all the land animals die? More importantly, as a carpenter, there is no way that Noah could have built the ark without help. This raises the distasteful possibility that Noah used hired help to complete the ark and watched as they died in the flood. This is morally distasteful. I don't believe that the Noachian Flood occurred and is simply a fabrication of history."

I reply, "When I brought ashore a couple of dozen fish, the twenty turned into fifty. Eventually this turned into hundreds and then thousands. Tell the story enough times and it assumes great significance. My crucifixion was eventful. This old woman gave me a cup of poison. It tasted bitter but I realized that she was trying to spare me the agony on the cross. Thankfully the poison killed me within hours. Shortly thereafter I found myself in the sarcophagus. When I met with God, he ordered me to return. Clearly my teaching must continue through your interpretation of my writings."

"By the way, are you reciting everything I say, or are you adding your own ideas?" I ask. "What's the matter, don't you trust me to be a faithful scribe?" Swadu inquires.

"I am concerned that you will interpret what I say and not record it faithfully," I reply.

"I am sorry, Jesus, but I have no faith in you. If you don't want me to be your scribe, find someone else." Now that was obnoxious!

"Would you like me to provide you with a miracle to convince you of my divinity?" I ask.

"How do you intend to do that?"

Time to teach this doubter a lesson! "Life is a circle, so I will set up a circle of straw. Roll a pebble along the circle a certain distance. Now count the number of lengths of straw it takes to get to the pebble in one direction. Then count the number of lengths of straw to get back to the beginning. How many do you count?"

"Five when I left and fifteen to return," he says.

"Now I will return to the circle and make it much larger. Count the number of pieces of straw again."

"It is ten to the start in one direction and twenty-five in the opposite direction."

"Life is an ever-expanding circle; as the world gets older, we are on a journey of an eternity. We are farther from the beginning and farther from the end with each step we take. God has designed this universe to have limited, but enormous, amounts of food, the physical world, and an infinite spiritual world. Just as God said he was the 'Alpha and the Omega,' we are trying to close the gap between us and Him. Whether we succeed or not, only God knows."

I continue, "As I indicated, the physical world is how God disposed of evil; merely turning it into the physical world. Thus the evil spiritual world goes through the guts of the physical world. As a result, good is increased gradually and the evil, physical world is steadily diminished. At some point in the future, everything evil will be brought into the physical world, and, over an eternity, it will be converted into the good, spiritual world. Little by little, evil evaporates; heaven will exist for an eternity and Satan, who thinks he is immortal, will die. This is his one recurring nightmare — the return to nothingness which, in some eastern religions, is nirvana."

This surprises Swadu. "But I thought that Satan, just like God, was immortal. How is this possible?"

"Because the circle of life grows forever and goes ahead and backwards, at some point the circle will be complete. As God and the Heavenly Host grow, Satan diminishes and eventually he becomes a memory."

"But won't that memory diminish Heaven?" Swadu inquires.

"Eventually the memory will cease to exist and all that is left is God," I conclude.

Swadu never gives up! "How can God forget?" This is getting annoying!

"He sleeps in nothingness, only to awake with a greatly weakened Satan as an opponent."

"Where is the miracle you promised me?" Swadu demands.

Now for some fun! "See the pebble? Now watch." I move my hand and the pebble begins to move slowly around the circle. Swadu gasps. Then I make it move faster and faster until it is a blur. Swadu says, "I am hallucinating; this can't be real."

"Would you like me to convince you it is real?"

"Please do so!"

I flick my wrist and the pebble flies out of the circle and strikes Swadu squarely on the forehead. Swadu gasps, "Ouch! Why did you do that?"

I laugh. "To defeat you is like David trying to defeat Goliath."

Thoroughly confused, Swadu weeps. "I don't know if it was real or a delusion."

It is time to hammer him when he is down. "Swadu, you don't fool me one bit."

This startles him. "Who do you think I am?"

"The one with many faces," I say. At this point, I notice an odd, red flash go through Swadu's eyes.

After regaining his composure, Swadu asks, "Do you consider yourself a God-fearing individual?"

That is a tricky question! After reflecting a little, I respond, "No. You can be either a God-fearing or a God-loving individual. You cannot be both."

I can tell Swadu thinks he has me, so he responds, "Why not?"

It is time to use logic against the supreme logician. "You cannot love that which you fear. If you love God, then His infinite love will wash over you. If you fear God, then you do not trust Him. It is clear that you expect mental or physical retribution from God. You cannot love such a God; that is why it is so difficult to love my Father. Women who are beaten in their marriages do not truly love their husbands because they cannot trust them. Beatings destroy trust and you cannot love someone you do not trust."

Seeing he has been beaten logically, Swadu switches course. "What will be the fate of the world?" He does ask good questions, though!

"That depends on the attitude of men and women. If they don't accept the existence of God and want miracles to prove His existence, then they may get more than they want. Perhaps there will be great physical calamities that have no known cause or great diseases striking without warning. Perhaps there will be a movement like yours to repeal the Ten Commandments and replace them with their own set of Commandments. God will not allow another Lucifer to occur, that is clear, but there will be those who wish to dominate others just like Lucifer. But when I return, it will not be as a vengeful God."

Genuinely impressed Swadu asks, "Out of the three virtues you claim are so important, which is most important: faith, hope, or love?"

"Faith; without faith, there is no way to know whether this reality exists or if it is just an illusion. Do you dream? Are the dreams real? Are the contents of those dreams real and an accurate reflection of reality? The secular world has faith in what they see around them; that it is real. The problem is this: As I've already stated, the physical world is based, in part, on evil. In other words the secular world bases its faith, in part, on evil. That is why God will not allow the secular world to achieve supremacy over the spiritual world.

"The physical world lies and lies and lies. To return to your original question, we do not know if we exist without faith. From faith stems hope and love. Although life is harsh, we must hope for a better world. The eons it will take for this to occur are more than the grains of sand in the sea. Those who lead a virtuous life will be rewarded, regardless of their faith. I fear that my followers will face stiffer opposition from those who don't care than from those that do. Those who don't care will deny the existence of God and preach the gospel of Man. When this happens, I will make my displeasure known. I will not allow the unbelievers to continue to corrupt the believers.

"Remember: Original sin was the use of logic to destroy faith. The unbelievers do not have the right to denigrate God in the presence of the believers."

Not entirely satisfied with this response, Swadu asks, "What would have happened if the physical world existed, but there was no spiritual world?"

I respond, "You ask a question that has no meaning. The physical world can exist solely to support the spiritual world; without creating life, God would have no reason to create the physical world."

Clearly, Swadu understands this and says, "Am I correct in assuming that the physical world without a corresponding spiritual world yields chaos?" Aha, he comprehends!

"Yes, you are correct; infinite chaos." It appears I am making progress with Swadu, and he asks a very important question: "How did God create the world in seven days?"

"Planning creation took seven days, but the implementation of that plan is ongoing. You will note that God created the heavens first. Why? Because God needed some place into which to put things. So out of Nothingness and Chaos, God created the heavens with nothing in them.

"Then he created the earth. The earth had no form. What does this mean? There was no recognizable shape to it. Then God said, 'Let there be light!' Before the creation of light there was nothing but blackness. This meant, 'Let there be light on earth.'

"God then said, 'Let there be a firmament in the midst of the water.' An interesting choice of words, as it implies, at some time, there was only water or only firmament. God continued, 'Let the earth bring forth grass.'

"This is necessary so animals have something to eat. Then God created whales, fowl, and all manners of things. Adam and Eve needed food. And then God created man and woman in his own image. This just means that God is both male and female or there are two Gods, one male, and one female, but I'm not sure of this. While God made Mary heavy with child, I believe that she may have also been far more than my mother. I wish I had known more about her before my crucifixion. Does this answer your question, Swadu?"

"Partially; but aren't you forgetting one important detail?"

Now I was intrigued. "What do you mean?"

Swadu had a smug look about him. "You will note that the heavens were created before the earth. Why? There was a need to create the heavens before putting something into it. Then God created the grasses so that animals would have something to eat, and the animals so that Adam and Eve had something to eat.

"What should be apparent is that the **order** of creation is as important as the **substance** of creation. In our world, God started out with lower forms of life and goes progressively to more complicated and sophisticated forms of life. To some, it would appear that, because God created Adam first, that He was to be given dominion over Eve. But why then, did God create Eve after He created Adam? She is the ultimate act of God's creation. Eve supersedes Adam. Dust is to Adam as Adam is to Eve."

I reply, "Doubt in the absence of God is faith. The meek shall inherit the earth. Women, and those who support them, shall inherit the earth."

Swadu asked, "Why didn't you tell this to your female prophets?"
"They already knew it."
Swadu was beginning to get frustrated. "When will misery on earth end?"
Finis! "When the lion lies down with the lamb."

Part II

Chapter 7

Suddenly a mob of villagers were in the valley below. I could see that they were heading towards the cave. As they arrived, I screamed at them, "Leave them alone. It is me you are after."

The last thing I remember is a rock hitting my head and falling down as a cart drove over my leg. I could hear the sound of screams from the cave and then, suddenly, the hillside collapsed on top of me. This time I was really dead.

Chapter 8

As the Cessna crammed with gear circles a small hill in the arid region below, the pilot, Jim, makes a brief comment to his beautiful copilot. "Ashley, you'll be in charge of groundtruthing A12 through A25. A25 looks like an artifact of the equipment. A cave that large would have been spotted centuries ago."

"Why must you be so negative, Jim?" asks Ashley. "Maybe it's the find of a lifetime.

"If it is, I'll streak the base camp at high noon on the day of your choosing."

"Remind me *not* to be there when you do that." Ashley says.

"What's fair is fair. If it's a bust, you will streak the base camp, right?"

"Sure; at midnight with a new moon."

As the plane swings into an arc, Jim and Ashley are treated to a beautiful sunset caused, in part, by a major sand storm a few days earlier. Jim, impressed by the beauty of the sunset, exclaims, "Don't you wish we could bottle this and take if back to Jerusalem?"

"If we did, there would be a fight over who owned it," Ashley replies.

"Now who's the pessimist?"

Chapter 9

Ashley is leading a group of assistants carrying picks, shovels, and dynamite along the base of the cliff. She is sweating profusely. She takes the back of her hand and wipes the sweat off her face with her sleeve. It leaves a streak of mud on her forehead. She is holding a map of some sort on the hood of a Land Rover. She is talking on the radio.

"Jim, Advance Camp 25 calling base camp. Do you read me; over?"

"What's up? Let me guess. Did you find a dozen mummies? Over."

"Nothing more than a talus pile beside the side of the mountain. What do you think your machine was reading? Over."

"Hard to say; maybe just some fluffy pyroclastics that give a false reading. Don't waste a lot of time there. Take some temperature measurements at different areas of the talus pile; we'll analyze them here. If there is a magician beneath the robes, we'll find him."

"You mean *her*," says Ashley. "Over."

At base camp, Jim and Ashley are reviewing the data from A12-A25. Ashley suggests, "A12-A18 look pretty normal. The thumper didn't pick up anything unusual. Temperature readings were within range. We didn't pick up very much there or from A19-A24. The sniffer picked up a little spike on A22, but it was a dead rat. A25 is intriguing. We couldn't use the thumper because it looked like the whole hillside might collapse. Even if we could use the thumper, the talus pile would prohibit cohesive passage of sound waves. The sniffer picked up a few indications of long strand hydrocarbons, but pretty much within background levels.

"Now for the intriguing part: We picked up slightly colder measurements of about three degrees at the base of the talus pile compared to the top of the pile, but this could be due to differential sunlight. Meaning there may or may not be a magician after all."

"I'm sorry, Ashley; it's pretty much a bust on this trip so far. We had better get very lucky very soon or our generous sponsors will pull our chain. Splat!

We go back to teaching the spoiled brats at Harvard. Go find us a magician," says Jim.

"Find us a magician, or invent a magician?" Ashley inquires.

"Whatever it takes."

Chapter 10

As she returns to A25, Ashley addresses ten of what appears to be graduate students. There are three Land Rovers and a big pile of equipment and digging tools.

"We've got a good jump on the day, but keep in mind that this talus pile looks pretty unstable; we are going to have to pull the blocks off the top." In her mind she muses, *I sure hope those temperature readings are for real and not some equipment error. It's the end of the expedition if the readings are wrong. I have an uneasy feeling about this place.*

"Start taking down the rocks at the top that look loose so that we can begin to work at the base," says Ashley.

The kids are hustling and bustling along, and they begin pulling rocks off the talus face. One young girl picks up a large, flat rock and screams as a snake strikes her in the face and falls backwards downhill. A shot is heard as a young man, Chris, tucks a pistol back in his belt after shooting the snake.

Ashley, scoffs, "Congratulations, Chris; it is a non-venomous whip snake. Come on people; the excitement is over. We have only seven more hours of daylight and a great deal of digging to do. Lucy, are you okay?"

"I'm fine, mom. The fall hurt more than the snake bite."

"Do you wanna rest?"

"No, Ashley, I'm fine."

As the dig progresses, the sun continues to slide across the sky. Two photographers take pictures as every rock is removed. At the end of the day, Ashley announces, "Whoever gets back to base camp first gets to take a two-minute shower. If you're last, you have to cook for three days."

As she steps into the driver's seat, the two male drivers get into their Land Rovers. "On the count of three: one, three." Ashley peals out and pelts the windshields of the other Land Rovers with gravel. Now begins a wild ride back to camp, highlighting Ashley's superior driving skills. Suddenly, she veers off the road and is airborne, slamming the frame of the Land Rover into the ground in a shower of sparks, but cutting about one hundred yards off the trip.

The two male drivers stay on the road. Ashley gets to base camp about thirty seconds before the second Land Rover arrives. Ashley walks along the road and sticks out her thumb like a hitchhiker; Sean stops to pick her up as the third Land Rover whizzes by.

"I always liked your cooking, Sean. You could use a little more training at Lime Rock." There weren't any pit bunnies like you at Lime Rock. You cheat really well," responds Sean.

"You mean the shortcut?"

"How did you find it?"

"Elementary, my dear Sean; just look at the aerials. If you had done your homework, you would have known what lays beyond the ridge; I cut off the curve in the road safely. If you would have had faith in me, you would have followed me instead of taking the wrong — excuse me, long way home."

Chapter 11

Jim is scanning the photographs of the day. There are several hundred of them. He slumps down in his chair and rubs his eyes. "Ashley, this looks like the ball game. I see nothing unusual in the graphs. Did you see anything unusual while you were there?"

"No, but I have a gut reaction that there is something there. Let me look at the photographs again."

"Be my guest."

Ashley sips a beer, then another, and another. By the time she is on her fourth beer, she shakes her head, peers at one photograph, rifles through her file, and compares it to a second. As she stares at it, she gets more and more animated. "Jim! Come here!"

Jim stumbles out of bed. "Wassup?"

"I've been comparing photographs from a one-meter grid near the base of the talus pile; look what I found! See this off white patch? It is only about two centimeters on a side. You will note when we had a small landslide and that the small, off-white object is gone. I missed it in the field."

"So what? It is probably a piece of quartzite. Forget it; we're going home," remarks Jim.

"Not yet; I want one more day in the field by myself, if necessary."

"You're drunk and on your own. The ship is sailing with or without you."

"You insufferable bastard. All I am asking for is one more day," says Ashley.

"That's not the way to get it. Our sponsors are breathing down my neck and want to cut their losses. What do you expect me to do? Okay; we'll wait to pack up camp and get to ready to leave. We'll continue to process the little data we have. Take Sean; you have one more day.

Chapter 12

As Sean and Ashley lie in bed together, she stares at the ceiling. She has on only a thin, form-fitting sheet covering her. It is clear from the sheet that she is moderately well-endowed. Then, unceremoniously, she jabs Sean in the side. "Wake up sunshine; let's roll."

Ashley dresses, starts coffee, and begins going to work on breakfast. By the time breakfast is ready, Sean arrives on the scene; it is still dark outside.

"Now you owe me breakfast *and* three days of meals," jokes Ashley.

"Have you forgotten? We leave tomorrow."

"Not tomorrow; I intend to find the magician."

They load their gear, get in the Land Rover, and head out at dawn. They head to the site with the sun barely showing in the east. Ashley pulls out the photographs with the white spot in them and then tries to orient herself with the photographs. She overlaps them to get an exact match. They are near the base of a major rock fall. Both Sean and Ashley are very careful.

Finally Ashley finds the right spot, except there is a large rock where the white object should be. She and Sean then proceed to roll the rock out of the way, only to find a layer of dust. Ashley gets out a whisk broom and dusts away the ash. The white object is indisputably bone.

She shrieks at the top of her lungs, "Yippee!" She and Sean do a little dance away from the find.

Sean asks, "Do we do a two meter or a three meter?"

"Three meter, if necessary; we will be her 'til dawn."

Ashley and Sean set up a square grid of nine feet by nine feet, with the bone squarely in the center. They use plumb bobs and levels in order to determine a horizontal surface. At two corners, they roll boulders out of the way so that they can put in stakes to define the grid; then they meticulously unearth the skeleton. They hook up a block and tackle to the Land Rove, using a fulcrum to pick the boulders off the skeleton. One of them reveals the mangled remains of a leg and foot. Another, a crushed torso and, still another, a crushed hand and arm. One arm with a hand and one leg with a foot are relatively intact. Beneath one boulder is a pile of partially burned material.

Sean asks, "Should we tell Jim?"

"Yeah, he will be pissed if we don't, and he has the entire camp broken down."

Ashley picks up the microphone to the radio. "Ashley calling base camp five; do you read me, Jim? Over?"

"This is base camp five. What is your status? Over."

In almost delirium, Ashley carefully disguises her emotions. "We have discovered a hominid about five feet ten inches tall beneath the talus pile. We expect to have the remains fully excavated within an hour. We request permission to stay the night in case marauders, human or otherwise. These jackals loot archaeology sites. They are not getting this one. Over."

"Great work, Ashley; I sure hope it wasn't some shepherd who died five hundred years ago. Over."

Ashley and Sean settle in for the night. They eat dinner together, but Ashley hears rustling in the scrub brush about one hundred yards away. She gets a gun out of the Land Rover and loads it. "Do you really think that's necessary?" asks Sean.

"Nothing is going to disturb the skeleton."

An Arab man asks, "Oh my pretty one; don't be afraid. We will gladly allow you to leave once we have found what you are hiding. You can only be guarding something of great value. Just leave and you can go unharmed."

"We have nothing of value here; please leave us alone!" responds Ashley.

Suddenly the windshield explodes next to Ashley. A split second later, a gunshot sounds. She hits the ground and crawls up to a large rock. She knows that there are at least two individuals she has to deal with; one to the side and one ahead of the Land Rover. "Do you think we should show them what we have?" asks Sean.

"Don't get silly now, Sean. They will kill us regardless of what they find. Now be quiet."

Just then a bullet ricochets off the boulder where she is talking to Sean. She immediately rolls to a second boulder. She sees a man running to the left. She explodes his right knee cap. He screams and falls to the ground. The instant Ashley fires the shot she immediately rotates ninety degrees and takes refuge behind another boulder. Within two seconds of Ashley hitting the first gunman, a shot hits the top of the boulder where she was a moment earlier. But now she can follow the flash of the gunfire to know where her assailant is located.

"Sean, can you get the night goggles out of the Rover?"

"I'll try."

"Just do it quickly." Sean crawls in the driver's side, flops over the seat, and starts rummaging through the supplies. After about twenty seconds, Sean says, "Got 'em."

He hands them to Ashley. "Come out, come out wherever you are," she says.

Another gunshot hits the Land Rover. Ashley has already fired off a shot toward the flash from the gun. She gets out the night goggles and sees a body sprawled over a boulder. "Sean, were there two or three of them?"

As she turns, the third man wraps a rope around Ashley's neck and begins to strangle her. "Where is the skeleton?" he demands.

Ashley backs up and stomps down on the intruder's instep so hard she breaks it. The man screams and let go of the rope. Ashley then knees him in the groin, and he collapses to the ground and begins moaning.

"Tie him up," she says to Sean. "I'll look out after the guy with the missing knee cap."

As she approaches her assailant, he pleads, "Please don't kill me! Please don't kill me!"

"Why not? You tried to kill us. Sean, we're going to have to stake turns putting pressure on the wound; otherwise this guy will bleed to death."

Chapter 13

It is daybreak at camp. The one intruder is carried out in a stretcher with an IV attached to his arm. The second assailant is hauled away by the police. Ashley dispassionately says, "We'll bury the other guy and get back to excavating the remains."

Ashley, Sean, and ten assistants return to the site and bury the body in a shallow grave. Then they return to the skeleton found by Ashley and Sean. "Did you bring the anoxic box in case we have flesh remaining from the skeleton?" Ashley asks.

Annoyed, Sean says, "Look; I know I don't meet your standards, but at least give me credit for preparing for the obvious."

"Sorry, Sean, but I feel this skeleton has a lot to offer us."

At long last they see the full extent of the skeleton. In the horizontal position to directly above the skeleton they see the skeleton in all its glory.

"Now that we are going to touch the skeleton for the first time, Sean, time to don the surgical gloves."

As they remove each piece of the skeleton, they take a picture and tag the bone. At long last, they get to the pelvic girdle and lift up.

Ashley shrieks, "There is still flesh here; Sean, get it quickly!"

Sean gets a pair of tweezers and quickly puts the flesh in the anoxic bottle for preservation. Ashley then speaks into a recorder and describes the events of the day so far.

"It looks like our magician is a male about fifty to sixty years old and in moderately good health. There is a peculiar indentation on one hand and one foot; cause unknown. The other hand and foot were crushed in the rock fall. The remains are tagged and secure. We are returning to base camp. That should get us funding for another year. Let's just hope it's not some five hundred-year-old shepherd who was in the wrong place at the wrong time."

"Jim, now it's time to earn your pay. See if you can get us some emergency funding."

"What do you propose I tell our sponsors? That a five-hundred-year-old year shepherd was crushed beneath the boulder? We need more. You've convinced me that we should have stayed the extra day. Now you've convinced me we can stay at least two more days."

"Jim, are you going to streak the camp tomorrow?" asks Ashley.

"Not yet; the jury isn't in."

Chapter 14

"Jim, before we begin anything, I propose we analyze the air currents in the debris pile. Kids, get out your notebooks and use matches to determine air currents. We'll start out ten feet apart. North is perpendicular to the cliff face. Try to determine which way the flame is bent; make a note of it every two feet or so, and we'll analyze this sucker. Don't leave burned matches on the ground."

A half hour goes by and Ashley collects all the data and plots it on a master chart. She spots a clear trend. Air is exiting at the bottom and entering at the top.

As a sign of authority, Jim announces, "No doubt about it; we have cold air exiting at the base and warm air entering at the top. It seems we have a large cave behind it. The day is toast; tomorrow we find out what lies behind the veil."

Chapter 15

Ashley snuggles up next to Sean in bed.
"Go away; you smell like a Billy Goat," he says.
"You sure know how to talk dirty. How about a shared sponge bath? Have you ever read the Kama Sutra?"
"And you have, I suppose?"
"Come on; you can teach me how to give sponge baths and I can teach you the Kama Sutra," she teases.
"That's a fair trade."
The two of them settle into a large tub and begin bathing each other and kissing passionately.
"What's the big deal about the Kama Sutra?" inquires Sean.
"When do we leave tomorrow?" she asks.
"About six o'clock."
"Can you get by on two hours of sleep?" she teases.

Chapter 16

"Jim, we are going to have to get several large boulders off the top of the pile. We'll need the winch for that. This is very dangerous. Be sure to let the setters get the chains in place before you start the winch," warns Ashley.

The winch operator nods in agreement. "Clear!"

Several graduate students run for the safety of the margin. The boulder bounces down the hillside and keeps going down the slope until it reaches the end of its play. The winch operator immediately senses extreme danger and dives off the truck. The split second after he dives off the truck, the wire pulls taut and the boulder rips the spool of wire out of its holder, and the spool rips off the top of the Land Rover where the driver was seated.

Disappointed, Ashley agrees with Jim. "That does it; we must use manual labor from now on to clear the rubble. It's slower, but less dangerous."

Several graduate students use a long board to get a twenty-ton jack under a large boulder. As they jack it up, they put shims under it and then reposition the jack for a better bite. After a while, the students are able to roll the boulder down the hill. Late in the day, the crew is able to open a small opening to what lies beyond. There is a general celebration.

"Ashley, it's getting close to nightfall; tomorrow is the big day. Pack up your gear and get ready for a long day tomorrow. I'll try to convince our sponsors to give us some breathing room," says Jim.

Chapter 17

Ashley is lying face down in the bed. Sean swats her on the ass.

"Wake up lazy bones; you don't want to miss the big day," he says.

"Don't play with the merchandise unless you tend to buy it. Could you hand me my robe?"

Sean leers at her. "Why don't you come and get it?" He holds the robe like a matador and starts walking toward the bed. Ashley lunges toward the robe.

"Give it to me you silly twit." She laughs as Sean throws it across the room.

"With the right persuasion, I could hand the robe to you, but I'd much rather watch you retrieve it."

Ashley raps the sheet around herself and fetches the robe. "Why are you so childish? You've seen me naked before."

"I was just refreshing my memory. Jeez, you have no sense of humor," jokes Sean.

"Au contraire; it is *precisely* because I have a sense of humor."

They gather at the site and Jim comments, "It's lucky we didn't dismiss this as a pyroclastic flow."

"You mean *I* didn't dismiss it as a flow," remarks Ashley.

"I stand corrected."

Ashley averred, "Based on the milligals, it's pretty clear that this cave is pretty good sized. I wonder what the shepherd was doing near the cave entrance? Wait a second; maybe we've got this all wrong. Could he be living in the cave? Can you spell artifacts? God, I have to wait to get back to the site. This could be the find of a lifetime."

"Or at least this week," Jim says sarcastically.

"Jim, you seemed awfully tired yesterday; why don't you stay here and get some rest? Your cynicism quotient is maxed out."

"Ashley, I appreciate your concern; I just don't want your expectations to embarrass reality. Let's get going. It is time to see if we have a magician beneath the robe."

Chapter 18

"Jim, we know we've got one skeleton. It's possible more may be inside the cave. Let's open her up."

All that separates the archaeologists from the interior of the cave is one, large boulder. The graduate students roll it down the hill.

"Jim, it's still too dark to see much. Lucy, please bring me a handful of glow sticks. We don't want to damage anything inside the cave with those bright lights. Jim, do you mind if I go in first?"

"It's yours, baby. Go ahead."

Ashley smiles and wriggles, feet first, into the opening. She finds a rock directly below the opening and stands on it. "Give me a couple of minutes to allow my eyes to adjust. The cave has a dirt floor. There seems to be some sort of wood framing. It looks like a cart. As far as the cave is concerned, the cross section is roughly thirty feet across with a ceiling of variable height; a good fifteen feet, I'd say."

Sean and Jim follow her into the cave. "Sean, you and Ashley study the walls, inch by inch; take respirators with you. If there are any cave paintings, we don't want to damage them. I'll take a quick look toward the back of the cave," says Jim. He inches toward the back of the cave, according to his tape measure.

Jim shouts, "Jackpot! We've got skeletons all over the place. Some died in each other's arms just like Pompeii. Screw the paintings; get the generator going and at least three hundred feet of cable."

Within minutes the generator is hooked up and cables are run into the cave. This is followed shortly by the glare of incandescent bulbs. Now the depth of the cave is apparent.

"Before anything else, Ashley, I think we will want a photomontage of the entire cave. Sequence your pictures at the entrance of the cave as North one hundred. Kids, it is time to do some mapping. Survey it first; run the levels next. Always be careful of where you place your feet. Let the photographer stay ahead of you. Ashley, you, Sean, and I will attempt to learn what we can before we begin processing the skeletons."

"Jim, do you think we should try to handle this many skeletons? It will be difficult to keep track of them all with our limited resources. I wonder why our first chap was running out of the cave," remarks Ashley.

"How do you know this?" says Jim.

"We found the body with the head facing down and the body aligned uphill from the head. In other words, it looked like he was facing down the hill. If he had been running uphill, his feet would point in a different orientation. That's strange. We may be wrong that the rock fall smothered these cave dwellers. Far more effective would have been for someone to drive burning carts of straw into the cave. The flames would have sucked out the oxygen in a matter of minutes. The residents would have sought refuge in the back of the cave, but it wasn't enough. Now the question is: What was Charlie doing running out of the cave and into the burning straw? We can only assume it was a desperate attempt to stop the invaders," says Ashley.

"Why did a group of individuals kill these cave dwellers? Were they robbers or outcasts? The most feared outcasts of the day were lepers. What did they do to antagonize the villagers nearby? I think that the answer is Charlie," responds Sean.

Somewhat bored by the commentary, Jim politely suggests, "Time to call it a day. Lyle, you, Angela, and Larry will stay here tonight. We'll provide you with all the supplies you need. I have to get back to camp to make a very important phone call. I suspect our sponsors will be delighted."

Chapter 19

The next day, the archaeologists begin the delicate task of wrapping the skeletons in shrink wrap and stabilizing them as much as possible by placing the bones in a cooler. It would be too risky to leave them in the cave.

"Jim, this is a tough call. Do we leave the skeletons here or take them with us? Now that they're exposed, it is best to try to preserve them in the lab. We'll stabilize them and isolate them from the elements in shrink wrap. That will take time," remarks Ashley.

The group watches as the archaeologists do their work, mapping the cave and preparing the skeletons for transport. On the final day, after everything but the camp is packed, they have a wild, drunken party; Ashley and Sean are trading shots.

"You know, Sean, I might have said yes if you'd ask me to marry you."

"Is it too late?"

"Just ask and see what happens."

Sean drops to one knee and kisses her boot. "Will you marry me?"

"If you tell me who Charlie is, I'll marry you." They look out the front flap of the tent to see Jim streaking the base camp. Ashley yells out the flap, "It doesn't count; it isn't high noon!"

The next morning, Ashley is examining the bodies in the crate. In her mind's eye, she remembers, but can't quite recall exactly, that something is out of place in the cave. She approaches Jim. "I think we may be missing something important in the cave."

"You'll have to wait until one season."

"Look, Jim, you gave me a couple of extra days and it paid off. I know that there is more to this cave than we've found. Do you want to risk that the robbers will get in there and find something we missed? Look what happened in Iraq. We are talking about the heritage of the Middle East; surely you can spare Sean and me with enough equipment and supplies to do the job."

"What do you hope to find?" Jim inquires.

"Serendipity."

Chapter 20

Ashley and Sean are in the cave. "What are we looking for, Ashley?"

"Anything out of place; let's start with the largest concentration of bodies. We assumed that they were trying to protect one another. What if they were trying to hide something? Wait one second. If Charlie is the key, maybe he was trying to convey something to the attackers."

"Like what?"

"We were assuming that the lump of charcoal we found near Charlie was from burning wood. What if it was parchment? Then there might be more. Clearly Charlie thought it was important, so maybe he has some more of it stashed away in the cave, away from prying eyes. What we should look for is one or more cavities in the rock; most likely at a height of six feet or below. Let's start at the back of the cave and work forward. We will start at the easterly side and work from there. Use the steel plate to make contact with the wall; if it is solid, it will ring. If it's hollow, it will make a dull sound."

"I think I can save us some time," responds Sean. "I took a couple of geology courses. Do you notice how this one rock on the wall looks out of place? The bedding is tilted at about a twenty-degree angle to the wall's bedding."

Ashley walks over and works on the rock to pry it free. She then gives it one last yank and pulls it out of the wall. They peer inside, but it is too dark, so she uses a flashlight and looks inside.

"Holy shit! We hit it! The mother lode!" screams Ashley. "Sean, it's time to don the surgical gloves. Can we carry all these? There must be several hundred! We have to get in touch with Jim!"

Ashley walks out of the cave and calls on the walkie-talkie. "Jim, do you read me? Over." The radio begins to make scratching noises.

A graduate student, Lyle, picks up the walkie-talkie and answers, "This is the rubber duckie. Over"

"Where the Hell is Jim?"

"Napping," he replies.

"Get the bloody twit on the talkie. Over."

"He's not bloody as far as I can tell. Over."

"Lyle, unless you want me to make your life miserable, I suggest you get Jim — *Now!* Over."

"Sounds to me like you're a real bitch when you're hung over, but I'll get Jim. Over."

Jim is groggy when he talks to Ashley. "This better be good. I was dreaming of eating caviar in a nice, warm bath. Over"

"Your bathtub is going to be made of solid gold."

"What did you find?"

"Just several hundred parchments. This looks like the Dead Sea Scrolls, part deux."

"Holy shit, you must be dreaming. How are we going to preserve them? This is going to have to be done with great care. We can't simply go to any university and ask for the means to preserve several hundred parchments. We are set up to preserve skeletons and minor amounts of paper. This vastly exceeds our ability to deal with it. If we contact Hebrew University, the Israeli Government will probably seize the documents and it might be years before we see them. We have to improvise something," says Jim.

"Jim, we have a few canisters of carbon dioxide. Maybe we can bleed the gas into a closed box with thermometers inserted in the box to see that the temperature stays around sixty degrees. That way, the positive pressure and the inert nature of the gas should preserve the parchment until we stabilize it. When we reach the airport, I'll alert the crew to the problem."

"We could transport this as medical supplies. You will have to grease the wheels to get this through customs," responds Ashley.

Part III

Chapter 21

Everyone is assembled in a classroom setting with an amphitheater facing the stage. Ashley, in attire suitable for a college professor, is showing scenes from Africa. "Do you know where the birth of our species occurred?"

A student, Lyle, raises his hand. "Africa."

"Where in Africa?"

"Old Forge."

General laughter erupts from the audience. "You mean Olduvai Gorge?" asks Ashley.

"Like I said, Old Forge."

One of the students raises her hand. "Why, Professor Seveille, when you know we all signed up for this course to hear about your discoveries two years ago, don't you fill us in?"

"That is not part of the course curriculum," responds Ashley.

Lyle speaks out, "I can't speak for the rest of the students, but I'd much rather you discuss our findings in the Middle East two summers ago."

"How many students would like to hear about my trip to the Middle East two summers ago?"

Every student raises their hand, and Ashley sighs, "We started out without knowing what to look for. We thought it might be possible to find rock shelters that had been missed by pot hunters. Much to our surprise, we found a cave in pristine condition in which all the inhabitants had been suffocated. We found one skeleton outside the cave, appearing to indicate the individual was running away from the cave. Carts of burning straw were shoved into the cave with the obvious goal of killing the inhabitants, but they caused the entire front of the cave to collapse, trapping the inhabitants inside and obscuring the cave until our team found it.

"We not only found the cave, but a cache of writings inside that is vast in extent. I am in the process of translating them now. We were able to use a programming technique that allows us to scan the scrolls using various wavelengths lengths of infrared radiation and unroll them electronically without actually unrolling them physically; this greatly reduces the degradation of the scrolls. From my preliminary analysis, they may be even more important than the Dead Sea Scrolls."

The next question hanging in the room is asked by Lyle. "How can you unroll the scrolls electronically?"

"Each character has a certain shape; each shape is composed of pieces. We simply photograph the scrolls as if we were peeling the bark off of a tree. Each layer has certain diagnostic features. We simply choose the most likely fit. It isn't perfect but it works. Using this technique, I have been able to translate about ten percent of the scrolls."

One of the students asks, "Who is the author?"

"We don't know, but he is brilliant."

The bell rings signifying the end of the class. "Class is over. May I see you Lyle for a minute?

"I know you are excited by this work, but I have to stick to the curriculum, so please don't bring it up in class. However, if you are interested, I need a lab assistant. Would you be interested?"

"Yes!"

"Follow me to my office, and you can fill out the paperwork."

"Thanks, Professor Seveille."

"Out of the classroom, you can call me Ashley."

"Thanks, Ashley."

Ashley, with Lyle in tow, enters her office. Ashley rummages through her cluttered desk and eventually finds the forms.

"May I see the skeletons?" asks Lyle.

Ashley chuckles, "Give me a little credit. Harvard has agreed to provide me with the necessary means to study the find offsite. One of the reasons I hired you is to go through the various research grants and suggest which ones I should act on and which I should axe."

"Where is the hidden laboratory?"

"The less you know the better."

There is a van parked down the street from her office, with what is clearly surveillance gear in the van. A voice from inside the van says, "The less you know the better." The operator of the equipment says, "Damn. She isn't ever going to tell us where the secret laboratory is."

As he speaks into a cell phone, he speaks in an annoyed tone of voice. "No good; she was just as uncooperative this time as always. Where could she be hiding the remains?"

Chapter 22

Ashley boards an Air Italia plane and, once she lands at the airport, she travels quickly to the Vatican. She is greeted by a Cardinal who embraces her warmly.

"Welcome to my favorite secularist. Did the trip treat you well, Professor Seveille?" "Very well, Cardinal Larke. How is the safe room progressing?"

"We have made it safe from everything except an atom bomb. When did you know you had found Christ?"

"When I began to translate the first documents, it was clear to me that this was no average individual. It was clear that Charlie — excuse me, I mean Christ — had been crucified, yet survived as evidenced by the growth of bone into the injured region. Jim was instrumental in getting the effects moved here. He is a good Catholic; I'm primarily interested in preserving the find for posterity."

"It seems rather cold to refer to Christ as a *find*."

"My apologies, your eminence. Here is how the remains of Christ wound up in your hands."

We see a flashback to the camp after the discovery. Ashley and Jim are at a bar when Ashley leans over to Jim. "You are a good Catholic; right, Jim?"

"How would you like to do for your faith more than any other individual has done?" "What are you babbling about?"

"Charlie is Christ," says Ashley.

Jim stiffens slightly, looks at her with incredulity, passes out, and then falls off the barstool. The commotion creates mild interest in the patrons who resume drinking. Ashley gets off her barstool and shakes Jim, who wakes up.

"Why are you telling me this? Don't you realize this will destroy the Catholic faith? Christ died for our sins. If he never died, the whole basis of Catholicism dies with his life."

"Then it is your job to convince the Pope that we have clear evidence he died and was resurrected. Can you do this?" inquires Ashley.

"I'll try to do this somehow. Why are you telling me this?" asks Jim.

"I know you have contacts in the Vatican; we need a safe haven and that isn't going to be in the States. We need a clandestine method of getting these skeletons and most of the parchment to the Vatican. I suggest we ship them by rail. We can have them shipped in storage so they won't deteriorate. Let me handle the logistics. Your bosses at Harvard may not approve of your decision. I'll deal with the administration."

"Do you wish to speak to the Pontiff?"

"Very much so. What should I say, or should I just listen?"

"Listen."

"Do you think that this will ever be made public?"

"Your job is to present it as a hoax. You realize that in order to avoid unnecessary disruption to Christianity, we must allow this material out in very measured steps. The masses are not ready for this and it would create massive disruption if it ever became common knowledge."

"Is the scientific community going to get to review this?"

"You are the scientific community. We trust your judgment."

"So far, no one has claimed the right to work on the skeletons. My official statement is that this takes time, as does the transcription of the scrolls. Harvard can play *dog in the manger* with the best of them. Just look at the Dead Sea Scrolls and how, for many decades, there was little cooperation between disciplines. With my find, little bits and pieces of the scrolls have come out, but nothing to connect the scrolls to Christ.

One of the things I am working on is a computer program to unwrap the scrolls electronically. By using low doses of infrared radiation, the dye warms up a fraction of a degree. We then take these hot spots and run them through a computer. It is sort of like a three-dimensional jigsaw puzzle. The computer makes a best guess by virtue of a three-dimensional grid, filling in the gaps when there is an overlap in the dye. With clever refinements in a few years, I predict we will even be able to see through one region of dye to the ones below it. If this technology is ever perfected, we could translate the entire batch within a week. Of course we won't do that. One thing seems clear: this Christ is far coarser and less *flowery* than the Christ we know."

"Surely you must know, Ashley, that Christ's teachings have been filtered down through many generations of scribes. Take for example when Christ starved himself for forty days and forty nights. When Satan appeared to him and offered him food, Christ is alleged to have said, 'Man does not live by bread alone.' Can we prove that he didn't say: 'I'm not hungry? The substance is there, but the exact phraseology may be different."

"Much as I would like to believe everything in the Bible is the word of God, I find the Gospels, in certain situations, to have internal conflicts that are tough to resolve. These scrolls should clarify the Bible quite a bit. How do you throw the bloodhounds off the scent? How are you going to falsify your own research?"

"A little contamination will do the trick," says Ashley. I intend to stumble onto some fourth-century ink that shows up on the scrolls that verifies their age. That, coupled with carbon fourteen dates from the parchment will prove the scrolls date from the fourth century. With a little more fudging, I can then bring their date of origin to the eighth century, degrading their significance."

"They would be of great value even then, but would have minuscule value compared to their dating to the time of Christ."

"Aren't you worried that the Pope will order their destruction to save Catholicism?"

"My gut tells me otherwise. Maybe you can float a story about these being writings of the Gnostics; that their writings are so controversial they would be disruptive to society so it is necessary to allow the interpretation of the scrolls in only small doses. What do you intend to do with skeletons?"

"We have retained some of the finest preservations in all of Europe. The body of Christ is another matter. I must confess that the Pontiff felt an overwhelming desire to touch Christ and, as he did, wept uncontrollably. But then, strangely, he laughed, as if exchanging a joke with an old friend. Then he ordered the skeleton of Christ be preserved."

"I'm off to Harvard. I have to try to understand Christ's writings. We have the entire set, crudely on computer, in the hopes to be able to translate some segments where the dye doesn't overlap. What is interesting or disturbing is that it looks like the scribe recording his writings had altered them deliberately. For example, we see more of the Old Testament, God style of writing in some of Christ's teachings. Was Christ trying to build a bridge between his Father and him?"

"That is difficult to say, but if you have any real evidence that the scribe was infusing his own ideas, that would be very troubling; not just for your findings, but for the entire Bible. It seems highly likely that the scribe would have been brilliant, too. Whether he would corrupt Christ's teachings deliberately is highly significant."

"Wish me luck. Bye."

Chapter 23

Ashley arrives at the airport and heads for Harvard. She gets to her office and finds the door ajar. She walks into the office.

"Lyle, are you there?"

She hears a noise and then whirls around, but a big man closes the door in back of her. She karate chops him on the neck, and he falls to the ground. He falls, but another man grabs her from behind. She tries to scream, but a third man puts a cloth over her mouth and, after a few seconds, she falls limp within his arms. A fourth man straps Ashley onto a gurney and attaches a fake I.V. to her arm. They wheel her out of the office just as Lyle arrives.

Lyle stops the men. "What's going on here?"

The intern holding the gurney replies, "Professor Seveille collapsed in her office, and we are taking her to Bellevue Hospital. You had better get in touch with the Administration so they can cover her classes. We'll meet you at Bellevue Hospital."

"I'll go with you," says Lyle.

"Unfortunately, we can't allow that. Just cover for Professor Seveille."

Lyle watches as the ambulance speeds off. He goes to the faculty lounge and tells another history Professor, Harry Rangle, that Ashley collapsed.

"Could you cover for Ashley for the three o'clock class?" asks Lyle.

"What happened?"

"Ashley collapsed and is being taken to Bellevue Hospital. We don't yet know what is wrong with her."

"Damn voice mail. Sean: I'm going to Bellevue to see how Ashley is doing. She collapsed in her office for some unknown reason."

Chapter 24

Ashley, who is blindfolded, is led to a small room with a bucket, a table, a chair, a set of pencils, and a notepad. Her handcuffs, her gag, and her blindfold are taken off. Three men leave the room and close the door behind her. A voice intonates from a microphone and we see that Ashley is being videotaped.

"What do you want?" asks Ashley.

"You know what we want."

"I'm not going to get involved in a guessing game."

"Oh my dear, Professor Seveille; you have already lost the game. Now tell us where the skeletons and the parchment are hidden, and you will die a painless death."

"What do you want?"

"What do you have of value, besides your life?"

"My work in the Middle East has no value to a non-scholar. This is not information that can be sold on the open market. If you obtain it, it will be of no use except to a collector. These are fourth-century artifacts that have no use except for posterity."

"You state that these are fourth-century artifacts. Why should we believe you?"

"What possible motive would I have to lie?"

"If you were protecting artifacts more valuable than fourth-century material." Ashley stiffens slightly. "Your demeanor betrays you, Professor Seveille."

"I was surprised that anyone would think that these were other than fourth-century materials," responds Ashley.

"Where are the skeletons and where are the artifacts?"

"Don't you think I will be missed?"

"You mean Sean? He can be of no help to you."

"The police and the FBI will be out in force looking for me."

"We will see. How long do you think you can go without sleep? Good night, Professor Seveille. Pleasant dreams."

The room is filled with flashing lights and a deafening sound. Ashley collapses to the ground and puts her hands over her ears. A shadowy figure — the "Voice" — emerges from a control booth. He consults with a woman we recognize as Lucy. "Are you sure these were no fourth-century artifacts?" he asks.

"Positive. Now will you release my mother?" Lucy says.

"Your problems are over. Put her in with her mother." The Voice nods to a thug, and he escorts her out. There can be little doubt as to her fate. The thug throws her in with Ashley.

"I'm sorry, mom; I told them the age of the artifacts."

Ashley slumps. "Now our days are numbered. Either we die or go insane."

Another man in the control booth says, "How long do you think it will take to break them? Sooner or later this joint will be raided."

The Voice states, "They will break one way or another."

"How long will that take?"

"A week, at most."

We see Ashley. She sits upright against the wall and begins to breathe rhythmically. We see a clock on the wall with six hours elapsing.

The door opens and a glass of water and a meal are left on the floor. The man says, "Here is food and drink." She just sits there. Then the man approaches her and shakes her. She lunges towards him, and he hits her on the head with the butt of a pistol. She falls down. He leaves.

When Ashley wakes up, she eats the food and drinks the water. "I saw your feeble attempt to escape. Surely you didn't think it would succeed!"

"I wonder if I could request some Mozart?"

"When you give us what we want, you can request anything you like — except your life. We might spare Lucy, provided you cooperate."

"You liar! You have no intention to release either one of us. We have nothing more to discuss."

The noise resumes. Ashley and Lucy sit against the wall, close their eyes, and their breathing lessens. The two men in the control booth talk about the women's personal hygiene. They speculate that the grunge factor will set in; meaning that their own filth will cause them to cave. "We must break them quickly," responds one of the men, but The Voice says, "Don't be ridiculous; these archaeologists can go for months not worrying about their personal hygiene. We may have to go to harsher forms of interrogation."

One of the thugs brings in their daily ratio of food. "Enjoy your daily repast. Never mind the maggots." The man removes the pail and puts another down. Each day, for seven days, the ritual continues.

Each day Ashley wakes up out of a trance and wolfs down her food, but only sips from the jug of water. She and Lucy look more and more disheveled. Ashley wretches into the pail, takes a drink of water, swishes it around inside her mouth, and then spits it out. She takes a long drink.

Chapter 25

We see an ambulance speeding away and Lyle's confusion. Lyle is absolutely devastated when he sees Sean. Sean and Lyle are at Bellevue. They speak to the attending nurse.

Sean asks, "Do you have an admittance form for an Ashley Seveille?"

"What is your relationship to her?"

"I am her fiancé."

"Let me check." She checks her computer. "I see no mention of an Ashley Seveille. Could she have been admitted under another name?"

"No."

"You could try Ellis. We had a big bus crash and our emergency room was swamped; she may have been taken to Ellis Hospital."

"Thanks; will try there."

Sean and Lyle run out to their car and rush to Ellis Hospital, where they run into the admitting office. "This is urgent. We are convinced my fiancé may have been kidnapped. Have you admitted an Ashley Seveille with the past few minutes?"

The nurse quickly checks the computer. "Nope."

Sean gets on the cell phone and dials 9-1-1.

"May I help you?"

"May I have the FBI? I need to report a potential kidnapping."

"I'll connect you."

The FBI operator says, "What is the nature of your call?"

"I am Sean Hannerty, and my fiancé may have been kidnapped. Four men wearing ambulance scrubs took her out of her Harvard office on a gurney. She is a professor there and has artifacts available to her worth millions. We were told that she would be taken to Bellevue Hospital. When we got there she hadn't been admitted. We were told to go to Ellis because the Bellevue emergency room was backed up; she was not admitted there either."

"I'll have an agent meet you at Harvard."

Sean, Lyle, and the FBI agent meet at the entrance to Ashley's office. Lyle opens the door for the agent. Lyle then says to the agent, "I didn't enter her office. I'll guess you will want a forensic team here."

"Lyle, what can you tell me about the four men and the ambulance? Focus on the ambulance."

"I can't remember much; I was too rattled."

"Ashley has probably been kidnapped by a foreign power that wants the chronicles and the skeletons. It is a long shot that she might have been kidnapped by a private collector. If it's a foreign power, then we're toast."

Sean looks dejected. He takes Lyle aside and whispers to him, "I must confide in you that we cannot reveal the true nature of the skeletons to the authorities because that would create an overwhelming uproar. If it has been done by a foreign power they can hide behind diplomatic immunity. Our only hope is that a private collector has Ashley and is trying to force her to reveal the location of the scrolls. It is possible she may already be dead."

Sean turns to the agent. "Her captors have at least a three-hour lead. My suggestion is that you check all vacant lots within a five-mile radius. They could not risk transferring her in a private car on the street. What her captors don't know is that we have implanted a computer chip in her scalp with a G.P.S. Since it has not been triggered, we must assume she is incapable of activating it. This is not a good sign."

"I believe her kidnappers will contact us with the threat to execute her if we don't provide the scrolls. I have no knowledge where the scrolls are, so we have no leverage. If we are lucky, it will be a private collector. I will inform the FBI of their names. These names can be cross checked with Interpol."

We are now in the FBI office with the FBI emblem on the floor.

Sean speaks to an agent. The agent says, "We know of a few, private collectors who could afford to hold these artifacts without selling them."

"Who are they?"

"The most likely bets are Clive Summerpoole, with an estimated worth of at least four hundred million dollars. The other is Harry Dubcek, with an estimated worth of over one billion dollars."

"Have either of these men had run-ins with authorities related to other artifacts?"

"None we are aware of. Wait a minute; I do remember Dubcek was involved with artifacts of a dubious provenance. I remember something to the effect that the Cairo Museum got a ten-million-dollar donation from an anonymous donor a few months later. The charges went away after a few years of litigation."

"Have you checked his mansion?" Sean asked.

"We took a look around the mansion and found nothing."

"I'm just going to nose around; nothing formal."

"Well, you know that would be illegal?"

"God only know what Ashley is going through right now."

There is a shot of Ashley and Lucy with their backs against the wall, with flashing lights and loud noises. Finally Ashley puts her hands over her head and trips the G.P.S.

"I'm sorry I didn't do this earlier; for all our misery we have learned very little about our captors. Try to remember what happens over the next few minutes. It is our only hope to learn what we can about our captors."

Sean instantly sees that the GPS has gone off and rejoices. The FBI immediately notes that the G.P.S. has gone off in a warehouse, over an hour's drive away. They notify the local police and speed off.

The Voice sees from his monitor that the police have arrived. "Ashley and Lucy, bye for now; it's been entertaining."

When Sean arrives, the police tell him that the warehouse has been abandoned. When they get to a far wall, Sean taps on it and discovers that it sounds hollow. He finds a piece of pipe and hits the wall, causing a slight tear. He continues to beat on the wall with extreme force until he creates a hole big enough to crawl through. The police try to pull him back, but he brandishes the pipe and orders them back. He enters the hole and finds a lit corridor. There he finds the control room with Ashley down below. He calls to her through the microphone. "Are you okay?"

"Is that you Sean?" responds Ashley.

"Hang in there!"

Sean heads into the room where he sees Ashley.

"I haven't brushed my teeth in over a w—." Sean kisses her on the mouth and pulls her into in an embrace that lasts minutes.

Chapter 26

The three of them: Ashley, Lucy, and Sean are at their apartment. Ashley steps out of the shower with a towel around her head, and she covers herself with a robe. Lucy is sitting on the bed in a bathrobe.

"This was clearly done by someone with money. This limits the potential prospects to someone who is rich and has a thirst for antiquities. But how could they know their true value? When they get them they could blackmail the Vatican."

"Mom, before they captured you, they threatened to kill you unless I told them the truth. They captured me in the field and, when I am in the field, I only call you every few weeks, so you had no idea I was missing."

Ashley, looking pensive, notes, "So the first round goes to our mysterious kidnapper. My guess is that he will not stop unless we stop him first."

We see the back of the head of one of the kidnappers as he is entering an Air Italia jet. The Voice says to an aide, "The Vatican is beautiful this time of year. Perhaps the Pontiff has some ideas about Professor Seveille's finds."